A Spoonful of Faith

To my dear sweet children, Layla and A.J., my
loving husband, and my parents and family,
who have all instilled in me different ways that
we can do *anything* with a little bit of faith.

A Spoonful of Faith

Copyright © 2022 by Jena Holliday

Special thanks to Terry Pierce and Luana Horry

All rights reserved. Manufactured in Italy.

No part of this book may be used or reproduced in any manner whatsoever without written permission except
in the case of brief quotations embodied in critical articles and reviews. For information address HarperCollins
Children's Books, a division of HarperCollins Publishers, 195 Broadway, New York, NY 10007.
www.harpercollinschildrens.com

Library of Congress Control Number: 2021933219

ISBN 978-0-06-301781-8

The artist used digital watercolor, pencil, and gouache brushes in Procreate to create the illustrations for this book.

Typography by Chrisila Maida

21 22 23 24 25   RTLO   10 9 8 7 6 5 4 3 2 1

First Edition

A Spoonful of Faith

Jena Holliday

HARPER
An Imprint of HarperCollinsPublishers

Layla was ready
for her first day of school!
But she was still nervous
to try something new. . . .

She went to the kitchen
to look for her mom.
'Cause mamas can help when
you need love and calm.

"Hey, sweetie, sit here. Let's make a quick meal that's full of good things to help how you feel."

"Whenever you're nervous
or worried or blue,
just one bite of this and
you'll see things anew."

She rushed to the cupboard
and took a long look.
Mama smiled when she found
her recipc book.

"To whip up some courage,
to make your own breaks . . ."

"... a **spoonful of faith** is all that it takes."

"When you're in a big group,
you might feel too small."

"But **dashes of kindness** can help you stand tall."

"When you give your best
but you keep hearing 'Nope' . . ."

". . . keep thinking good things and add *handfuls of hope*".

Then Layla broke out into a confident grin.

"Add **pinches of prayers** and **warm hugs** to whisk in."

But suddenly Layla
looked down at the bowl.
"Mama, where is it?"

Then deep in her soul . . .

. . . she knew.

The treat is *God's love!*
It was there from the start.
"Oh, Mama, I feel it
deep down in my heart."

"I'm ready," said Layla,
"to try something new!"

"With a spoonful of faith . . ."

"... watch *all* I can do!"

When I was a little girl, I lived by the idea that "you might as well think big." It never made sense to me that anyone *would* think small. That's why you'd always find me filled with big ideas of things I wanted to do! And, luckily, my parents encouraged it. My dad taught me that if I believed enough and had faith, it could change things. My mom instilled the importance of owning my uniqueness as a young Black girl and what I had to offer the world.

As those ideas marinated in me over the years, the words *spoonful of faith* fell on my heart one day and never left. That little sip of faith led me to start sharing my doodles, and I eventually became a professional illustrator! It sounds crazy(!) but believing in hope and having faith has always been medicine for me—a comfort—and it can work wonders for your courage and your heart. I'm a living example.

Let this story be a reminder to take some with you! With a spoonful of faith, who knows what you'll accomplish in the world around you.

Jena Holliday

Jena (pronounced jee-nuh) Holliday is a children's book creator, graphic artist, wife, mother, and believer. While previously working in the marketing field, God showed up, and, in a beautiful way, merged her love of storytelling with her passion for art, and the Spoonful of Faith brand was born. Jena lives in Minneapolis, and you can visit her at www.spoonfuloffaith.com.